George Cockburn

Extract From a Diary of Rear-Admiral Sir George Cockburn

with particular reference to Gen. Napoleon Buonaparte, on passage from

England to St. Helena, in 1815. On board H. M. S.

George Cockburn

Extract From a Diary of Rear-Admiral Sir George Cockburn
*with particular reference to Gen. Napoleon Buonaparte, on passage from England
to St. Helena, in 1815. On board H. M. S.*

ISBN/EAN: 9783337103729

Printed in Europe, USA, Canada, Australia, Japan

Cover: Foto ©Raphael Reischuk / pixelio.de

More available books at **www.hansebooks.com**

Extract from a Diary

OF

REAR-ADMIRAL

SIR GEORGE COCKBURN,

WITH PARTICULAR REFERENCE TO

GEN. NAPOLEON BUONAPARTE,

ON

Passage from England to St. Helena, in 1815.

ON BOARD

H.M.S. "NORTHUMBERLAND,"

Bearing the Rear-Admiral's Flag.

- - -◆- -

PRICE TWO SHILLINGS.

—◆—

London:—SIMPKIN, MARSHALL & Co.
1888.

PREFACE.

The M.S. from which this "Extract" has been printed, was found, in his own handwriting, among the papers of my late father; attached to it being a note, also in his own handwriting, to the effect that it is a reproduction of a copy found at St. Helena, in 1824 or 25, among the effects of one who had held an official position as Admiral's Secretary or Captain's Clerk on board the "Northumberland" on her voyage to St. Helena, where he died, and who had no doubt made it as a matter of pardonable curiosity and satisfaction for himself; and it is now published in the belief that it's intrinsic interest, as closing a gap in the later career of the great soldier, will be deemed sufficient excuse for it's seeing the light.

THOS: SALKELD BORRADAILE.

Surbiton, 1888.

Extract from a Diary

OF

REAR-ADMIRAL SIR GEORGE COCKBURN.

O N the *6th August*, being off the Start in the "Northumberland," I met Lord Keith in the "Tonnant," having with him the "Bellerophon" and some frigates in which were General Buonaparte and all his suite. As the removal of the General and his things was likely to occupy some time, and the doing of it with the ships under sail might be attended with inconvenience, Lord Keith agreed with me in the propriety of anchoring the whole off the Berry Head, which was accordingly done the same evening; and his lordship afterwards accompanied me on board the " Bellerophon " to make known to General Buonaparte that in pursuance of instructions under which I was acting, he, the General, was to be removed as quickly as convenient into the " Northumberland " for the purpose of being conveyed to St. Helena. The General protested very strongly against this proceeding and against the right of the British Government thus to dispose of him. Very little other conversation passed between us; we did not think it necessary to enter into the merits of the question with him, but contented ourselves with observing that, as military officers, we must, of course, obey the instructions of our Government, and therefore that we hoped he would be ready to remove to the " Northumberland " the next morning.

On the *7th August*, after breakfast, I went again to the " Bellerophon " to examine the baggage, &c., of the General and of those who were to accompany him, at which he was extremely indignant. I, however, in conformity with my instructions, caused everything to be inspected previous to permitting it to be sent on board the " Northumberland;" all the arms of every description were delivered up by him and his suite, and I stopped 4,000 napoleons in gold, which I delivered to Captain Maitland to be by him transmitted to the Lords Commissioners of the Treasury. Everything else belonging to them being transhipped and the necessary arrangements completed, about midday Buonaparte embarked on board the " Northumberland," with the persons undermentioned, viz.—

Grand Maréchal Comte de Bertrand.
  Madame de Bertrand.
  3 children of ditto.
  1 female servant with her child.
  1 man servant.

General Comte de Montholon.
  Madame de Montholon.
  1 child.
  1 female servant.
Le Comte de Las Cases.
  1 son (a boy about 13 years of age).

General Gourgaud.
  3 valets de chambre.
  3 ditto de pied.
  1 maitre d'hotel.
  1 chef d'office.
  1 cook.
  1 huissier.
  1 lampiste.

Of which—

  7 grown-up, to be at my table.
  2 maid servants
  1 young gentleman } at a separate table.
  5 children
  12 domestics, with my servants.
  ___
  27 in all.

On reaching the deck he said to me, "Here I am, Admiral, at your orders!" He then asked to be introduced to the Captain, then asked the names of the different officers and gentlemen upon deck, asked them in what countries they were born and other questions of such trifling import, and he then went into the cabin with Lord Keith and myself, followed by some of his own people. After I had shown him the cabin I had appropriated for his exclusive use and requested him to sit down in the great cabin, he begged me to cause the Lieutenant of the ship to be introduced to him; as, however, at this time his own followers came to take leave of him, I thought it best to leave him for a little while to himself, and I found soon afterwards advantage was taken of this for him to assume *exclusive* right to the after, or great cabin. When I therefore had finished my letters I went into it again with some of my officers and desired M. de Bertrand to explain to him that the after cabin must be considered as common to us all, and that the sleeping cabin I had appropriated to him could alone be considered as exclusively his. He received this intimation with submission and good humour and soon afterwards went on deck, where he chatted loosely and good-naturedly with everybody.

At dinner he ate heartily of almost every dish, praised everything and seemed most perfectly contented and reconciled to his fate. He talked with me during dinner much on his Russian Campaign, said he meant only to have refreshed his troops at Moscow for four or five days and then to have marched for Petersburg, but the destruction of Moscow subverted all his projects, and he said nothing could have been more horrible than was that campaign; that for several days together it appeared to him as if he were marching through a sea of fire owing to the constant succession of villages in flames which arose in every direction as far as his eye could reach ; that this had been by some attributed to his troops but that it was always done by the natives. Many of his soldiers however, he said, lost their lives by endeavouring to pillage in the midst of the flames. He spoke much of the cold during their disastrous retreat, and stated that one night, after he had quitted the army to return to Paris, an entire half of his Guard were frozen to death. He also told me in the course of this evening that previous to his going to Elba he had made preparations for having a Navy of 100 sail of the line; that he had established a conscription for the Navy, and that the Toulon Fleet was entirely manned and brought forward by people of this description; that he ordered them positively to get under weigh and manœuvre every day the weather would permit of it, and to stand out occasionally and to exchange long shots with our ships; that this had been much remonstrated against by those about him and had cost him at first a good deal of money to repair the accidents that occurred from the want of maritime knowledge, such as from the ships getting aboard of each other, splitting their sails, springing their masts, &c., but he found that even these accidents tended to improve the crews and therefore he continued to pay his money and oblige them to continue to exercise. He said he had built his ships at Antwerp in rather too great a hurry, but he spoke highly in praise of the port and said he had already given orders for a similar establishment to have been formed on the Elbe; and had fortune not turned against him he hoped to have sooner or later given us some trouble, even on the seas. He stated that the reason he had over-hurried the ships at Antwerp, before mentioned, was because he was anxious to press forward an expedition from thence against Ireland. After taking his wine and coffee he took a short walk on deck and afterwards proposed a round game at cards; in compliance with which we played at vingt-un until about half-past ten, won from him about seven or eight napoleons, and he then retired to his bedroom, apparently as much at his ease as if he had belonged to the ship all his life. I afterwards disposed of his whole party for the night, though not without some difficulty; the ladies with their families making it necessary I should provide them with adequate room and accommodation, and yet each other person of the suite asking for and expecting a separate cabin to sleep in and in which to put their things.

On the *8th August*, we lay-to the most of the day off Plymouth, waiting to be joined by the squadron destined to accompany us. It had blown fresh during the night, which left rather a heavy swell, the effect of which prevented General Buonaparte from preparing for dinner (at least that was the excuse made for his non-appearance), and I consequently did not see him during the day.

On the *9th August*, being joined by all our squadron (except the " Weymouth " which I could not wait for), we proceeded on our way down Channel, with tolerably fine weather but wind from N.W. General Buonaparte came out of his cabin, for the first time this day, about two p.m. and took a short walk on deck, but as I was busy writing I did not see him until dinner time. I found him rather lower and more reserved than the first day; indeed, until after drinking a tumbler of champagne he hardly spoke at all, but afterwards he conversed with more freedom, and made many and particular enquiries on the number and state of our forces in India; said he had been in correspondence with Tippoo Saib, and that he had hoped to have reached India when he went to Egypt, but the removal of the Vizier, and the alteration of politics of the Ottoman Porte, with other circumstances, had prevented his pursuing the career there which he had at first contemplated. After dinner he went upon deck, and persisted in keeping off his hat as he walked up and down, evidently with a view to inducing the English Officers on deck also to continue uncovered (as his French attendants did, and as I am told the Officers of the

" Bellerophon " used to do whilst he remained on the deck of that ship). Observing this, I made a point of putting on my hat immediately after the first compliment upon going out, and I desired the Officers to do the same, at which he seemed considerably piqued, and he soon afterwards went into the cabin and made up his party at vingt-un, but he certainly neither played nor talked with the same cheerfulness he did the first night : this might, indeed, have been accident, but it appeared to me to proceed rather from downright sulkiness, though I cannot but remark that his general manners, as far as I am yet able to speak of them, are uncouth and disagreeable, and to his *French friends* most overbearing if not absolutely rude. About eleven he retired to his bedroom, having been as unfortunate at his vingt-un party as the evening before. (Just before dark this evening I dispatched a brig to put letters into the Post Office at Falmouth, off which place we were, to inform Government of our progress.)

On the 10*th August*, as soon as the brig I had sent to Falmouth rejoined me, we made sail on the starboard tack, the wind being still from the westward with considerable swell from that quarter. Buonaparte did not make his appearance until just before dinner, when I found him playing at chess in the great cabin with the Comte de Montholon. He appeared to me to play but badly, and was evidently inferior to his antagonist, who I observed nevertheless was quite determined not to win the game from his ex-majesty.

At dinner, Buonaparte told me, when talking about our late contests with America, that Mr. Maddison was too late in declaring his war, and that he never made any requisition to France for assistance; but that he (Buonaparte) would very readily have lent any number of line-of-battle ships Mr. Maddison might have wished for, if American seamen could have been sent to man them and carry them over ; but that the affairs of France beginning to go wrong about that period, it was out of his power to afford any other material assistance to the American Government.

Immediately after dinner to-day, the General got up rather uncivilly and went upon deck as soon as he had swallowed his own coffee and before all the rest of us were even served. This induced me to request particularly the remainder of the party to sit still, and he consequently went out only attended by his

Maréchal, without the slightest further notice being taken of him. (It is clear he is still inclined to act the Sovereign occasionally, but I cannot allow it, and the sooner therefore he becomes convinced it is not to be admitted the better.)

General Gourgaud (who was in the Battle of Waterloo) told me to-day that during that battle, when the Prussians appeared, Buonaparte believed them to have been General Grouchy's Division, he having left between 30 and 40,000 men with that General, under orders to advance (in the same direction from which the Prussians had come) if from the firing heard General Grouchy should have reason to suppose the day was obstinately contested by the English; and this, he said, induced Buonaparte to persist in his efforts so long, and occasioned (when it was discovered that there were nothing but Prussians on the French flank) so general and complete a rout.

He said Buonaparte was forced off the ground at last by Soult, and he proceeded afterwards as quickly as possible to Paris; but so great was the panic and disorder among the French soldiers, that many of them (without arms or accoutrements) actually arrived in Paris (some

behind carriages, others in carts, &c.), on the
same day with the General and his attendants,
not having halted once from the moment of
their quitting the field, and reporting everywhere as they passed that all was lost. So
well do these soldiers seem to have followed
their chief's example in the hour of difficulty
and danger ! ! !

Our latitude this day at noon was 49° 41' N.

On the 11*th August*, it blew very fresh all
day from the N.W., and I was forced to carry
sail to weather Ushant, which occasioned all
my French party, from the master to the man,
to be miserably sick; I therefore saw nothing
of General Buonaparte throughout the day. I
had, however, some conversation with M. de
Bertrand, which tended to prove to me how
blindly attached he is to Buonaparte, and
how decidedly inimical to the Bourbon family.
He affirmed that neither Ney, nor Soult, nor
any of the French maréchals were apprised of
Buonaparte's intention of returning from Elba
to France; that it was adopted by the General
of his own accord, in consequence of his
observing in the public papers how unwisely
the Bourbons were acting, and which rendered
him certain how unpopular they would be

throughout France, and consequently that he
(General Buonaparte) had only to shew himself
there to be joined by everybody ; but to the
moment of his actually landing in France,
he had not received a promise or a line from
anybody with proposals or recommending the
step. M. de Bertrand told me they landed
with only 600 men ; that he was sure Ney left
Paris with the intention of obeying the king's
orders and opposing Buonaparte's progress ;
but finding the soldiers he commanded, and
indeed almost all his officers, resolved on joining Buonaparte instead of acting against him,
he (Ney) then determined on taking the same
line, as the only way of keeping the command
of his division ; and after having so resolved,
he thenceforth acted most zealously for the
new cause he had adopted, and did everything
in his power to forward Buonaparte's views,
and thwart and destroy those of the Bourbons.
Bertrand then added that General Buonaparte
was received everywhere, as he advanced in
France, like a father returning to his children,
and that he would be always so received again
in the event of his landing there (after the allied
troops had quitted the country) owing to the
love and affection borne him by every individual

in the country. I could not help smiling at this statement of M. de Bertrand's, and asking him, in reply, if Buonaparte were so popular with all descriptions of persons throughout France, why he had so quickly determined on quitting it altogether after the defeat of Waterloo, instead of endeavouring to rally the dispersed armies, and make further efforts to defend the country? The only answer I could get from him to this question was, that General Buonaparte had expected to have been very differently received by the English; and that he had been much influenced in taking the step he had done by the Abbé Sieyes, who had strongly advised the General to proceed at once to England in preference to taking any other course.

Our latitude and longitude this day at noon were 48° 48' N., 5° 58' W.

On the 12th August our weather was more moderate, though the west wind and swell continued. Buonaparte came upon deck this day earlier than usual, that is to say about three o'clock. He does not generally quit his bed till between ten and eleven, and, like most Frenchmen, he breakfasts, reads, &c., before he makes his toilet, but he does not come out of his own cabin until he is dressed. He appeared to-day thoughtful and low, though in good health. I had a tolerably long conversation with him relative to Ferdinand of Spain: he said he considered him to be both a fool and a coward; that he was now perfectly under the dominion of the priesthood and was merely a passive instrument in the hands of the monks; he added, he looked upon King Charles of Spain as an honest good man, but that he had lost everything by his attachment to a bad wife.

He told me that Baron de Kolly, who was sent by our Government to bring off Ferdinand, was first found out by his endeavouring to gain some person to his interest in Paris, as also from suspicion excited by the command of money which he appeared to possess; that upon his being arrested all his papers were discovered, and then that it was determined to send off a police officer from Paris to personate Kolly at Vallançay, to deliver the Prince Regent's letter, and to assure Ferdinand that everything was prepared for his escape, purposely to prove how he would act under such circumstances; but in spite of everything this sham Kolly could urge (and Buonaparte added

B

that he was a clever fellow) Ferdinand's·
courage was not equal to the undertaking,
and he obstinately refused to have anything
to do with the supposed agent of Great Britain.
The General assured me that until Kolly was
discovered at Paris the French Government
had no idea of our attempting to carry off
Ferdinand, but, however, that he was quite
convinced, had Kolly not been discovered, that
the pusillanimity of Ferdinand would have prevented all possibility of our success. I told
him we had some suspicion of Baron de Kolly
having played a double part in the transaction,
but he said upon his honour it was no such
thing.

Speaking of Captain Wright, he said that
when Lord Ebrington, at Elba, first drew his
attention to the name and to the circumstances
respecting Captain Wright he did not recollect
the case, which, he said, was exactly this; that
Captain Wright, being supposed in France to
have been concerned with the conspiracy of
Georges and others, was, when taken, conveyed
to the Temple preparatory to being examined
with reference to that transaction, and on
being ordered to attend a council charged with
the investigation of it, he had *put an end to*

himself. Buonaparte, though he confessed he could not give any reason for Captain Wright committing such an act, yet added that the inferior rank and little consequence of this officer ought to have exempted him (Buonaparte) from the charge of having either ordered or attached any importance to his death.

He asked me during this day's conversation a good many questions respecting the Spanish-American Colonies, and said he thought Spain would, by the present bigoted misconduct of Ferdinand, infallibly lose them all.

In the evening he played at vingt-un as usual until about eleven, but he did not seem to recover his spirits; he talked but little and appeared much absorbed in thought.

This day at noon we were in latitude 46° 30' N., longitude 8° 2' W.

On the 13*th August*, it was calm most of the twenty-four hours, but still we were attended by a disagreeable swell. I did not see much of General Buonaparte throughout this day, as owing to his appearing inclined to try to assume again improper consequence, I was purposely more than usually distant with him, and there-fore, though we exchanged common salutations and *high looks*, nothing passed between us worth noticing.

Our latitude and longitude to-day at noon were 45° 42' N., and 8° 10' W.

On the 14th *August*, we had a continuation of fine weather and light winds. The General and myself were again distant and high with each other, though perfectly civil—at least he has been as much so as his nature (which is not very polished) seems capable of—and his attendants are certainly behaving as if anxious to gain my good opinion.

Our latitude and longitude to-day at noon were 45° 13' N., 9° 5' W.

On the 15th *August*, we had still light winds and fine weather with less swell than usual, which may in some measure account for General Buonaparte being more sociable and apparently more at his ease. It being his birthday I made him my compliments upon it and drank his health, which civility he seemed to appreciate; and after dinner I walked with him on deck and had rather a long conversation with him, in which I asked him whether he really had intended to invade England when he made the demonstration at Boulogne. He told me he had most perfectly and decidedly made up his mind to it, but his putting guns into the praams, and the rest of his armed

flotilla, was only to deceive and endeavour to
make us believe he intended to attempt making
a descent on England with their assistance
only, whereas he had never intended to make
any other use of them than as transports; and
he had entirely depended on his fleets deceiv-
ing ours by the routes and manœuvres he
directed them to make, and that they would
thereby have been enabled to get off Boulogne,
so as to have a decided superiority in the
Channel long enough to ensure his making
good his landing; for which he said everything
was so arranged and prepared that he would
only have required twenty-four hours after
arriving at the spot fixed upon. He said he
had 200,000 men for this service, out of which
6,000 cavalry would have been landed with
horses and every appointment complete, fit
for acting the moment they were thrown on
shore; that his praams were particularly
intended for the carrying over these horses.
He told me the exact point of debarcation had
not been fixed upon by him, as he considered it
not material and only therefore to be determined by the winds and circumstances of the
moment; but that he had intended to have got
as near to Chatham as he conveniently could,

to have secured our resources there at once, and to have pushed on to London by that road. He said he had ordered his Mediterranean Admiral to proceed with his fleet to Martinique to distract our attention and draw our fleets after him, and then to exert his utmost efforts to get quickly back to Europe; and, looking into Brest (where he had ordered another fleet under Gantheaume to be ready to join him), the whole was to push up Channel to Boulogne, where Buonaparte was to be ready to join them and to move with them over to our coast at an hour's notice; and in point of fact, he said, he *was so ready*, his things embarked and himself anxiously looking for the arrival of his fleets, when he heard of their having indeed returned to Europe, but that instead of coming into the Channel in conformity with the instructions he had given, they had got to Cadiz, where they were blockaded by the English Fleet, with which they had a partial engagement off Ferrol; and thus, he said, by disobedience and want of management of his Admiral, he saw in a moment that all his hopes with regard to invading England were frustrated, with this additional disadvantage (which he had fully foreseen when he first turned in his mind the idea of such attempt), that the preparations at Boulogne had given a stronger military bias to every individual in England, and enabled ministers to make greater efforts than they otherwise perhaps would have been permitted to do. He added that he believed, however, the English administration had entertained great alarms for the issue if he *had* got over, as his secret agents at the Russian Government reported to him that Great Britain had most pressingly urged that Court, with Austria, to declare war against France for the purpose of averting from England the danger of this threatened invasion; which he said, however, he had given up from the moment he found his fleets had failed him, and, having then turned his whole attention to his new enemies on the Continent, his forces collected at Boulogne enabled him to make the sudden movement which proved fatal to General Mac, and gave him (Buonaparte) all the advantages which followed. In short, the account he gave me very much tallied with Goldsmith's relation of the same circumstances (as given in his secret History of St. Cloud), and I must say, from what I have hitherto seen and learned, I begin to think Mr. Goldsmith had more foundation for many of his statements than he has generally received credit for. Buonaparte, however, told me in a manner not at all suspicious that Admiral Villeneuve decidedly *put himself to death*, though the General, in talking to me of him, seemed very strongly impressed with an idea of the Admiral's unpardonable disobedience and misconduct throughout. He also told me that he had ordered Admiral Dumanois to be tried by a court martial for his conduct at the Battle of Trafalgar, and that he had exerted all his influence to get him shot or broke, but that he had been acquitted in spite of him; and he added, when the sentence of acquittal was given, Admiral Cosmas (who was one of the Members of the Court, and who he said he decidedly considered to be the best sea officer now in France, and who has therefore been lately created a peer) broke his own sword at the time that of Dumanois was returned to him; which act Buonaparte seemed to have been most highly pleased with, and which was most probably the real cause of Cosmas's advancement to the peerage.

In the course of this evening's conversation he informed me that he had prepared a strong expedition at Antwerp, destined to act against Ireland, which he had only been prevented from sending forward by his own affairs beginning to take an unfavourable turn on the Continent.

His spirits throughout this day appeared considerably better than for some days past; he won a good deal at vingt-un, and his good fortune seemed to gratify him, the more as it was his birthday. He did not go to his bedroom this evening until past eleven o'clock.

Our latitude and longitude this day at noon were 43° 51' N., and 10° 21' W.

On 16th August, we had a continuation of fine weather, but light winds with calms. General Buonaparte is, I am glad to observe, evidently improving in his spirits and his behaviour, and as I am always ready to meet him half-way, when he appears to conduct himself with due modesty and consideration of his present situation, after dinner to-day I had a good deal of pleasant conversation with him; in the course of which some of the most remarkable circumstances he mentioned were, he assured me upon his word and honour (as

Comte de Bertrand had done before), that he had not any communication or invitation from any of the Maréchals or Generals, or from any other person in France, when he returned to it from Elba, but that the public papers conveyed to him such an acccount of the state of France as induced him no longer to hesitate in taking the step he did : that on his getting within about five leagues of Grenoble, soon after his landing in France, a detachment of troops of the 3rd Regiment showed inclination to resist him ; that he put himself immediately in front, and throwing open his great coat to shew himself more conspicuously, called to them to kill their Emperor if they wished it ; that this had the effect he expected, and they all immediately joined him ; and afterwards he received nothing but congratulations and proofs of attachment all the way to Paris.

He said, at Paris he had paid too much attention to and submitted too much to the opinion of the Jacobin party, which he now was persuaded had not been so requisite for him as he had conceived it to be, and that he should have done better if he had taken his measures from himself, and depended on his own popularity. He said the conduct of the allies obliged him to form his army, and move it, so quickly that he had not time to examine it and weed it as he should have done, and therefore many officers remained in it who had received their appointments from the Bourbons, and were extremely disaffected to him and anxious for opportunity to betray him. He said that he did not lose any soldiers from desertion on his march, but that his officers were constantly deserting. He then paid a compliment to the lower order of people in France at the expense of the higher orders. He said the former were the most sincere, the most firm, and at the same time the best dispositioned people in the world; but in proportion as you rose in class of people in France, the character became worse, and above the bourgeois they were too fickle and too volatile to be at all depended upon; they had one principle for to-day, and another for to-morrow, according to the circumstances of the moment; and he attributed solely to the disaffected officers of his army his Waterloo disasters. He contradicted what General Gour-gaud said the other day respecting his having mistaken the Prussians for General Grouchy's division, and assured me he knew early in the day the Prussians were closing on his flank; that this, however, gave him little or no uneasiness as he depended on General Grouchy also closing with him at the same time, and he had ordered a sufficient force to oppose the Prussians, who were in fact already checked; and he added that he considered the battle to have been upon the whole rather in his favour than otherwise throughout the day, but that after dusk the disaffected officers he had alluded to promulgated the cry of "*sauve qui peut*," which spread such confusion and alarm throughout his whole line, that it became impossible to counteract it, or to rally his troops, situated as they were; though he said had it been daylight, he was positive the result would have been different, as he then would only have had to have placed himself in a conspicuous situation in the front to have insured the rallying of all his troops around him, but, as it was, treachery and darkness combined rendered his ruin inevitable.

He said he did not on the morning of the 18th June entertain the most distant idea that the Duke of Wellington would have willingly allowed him to have brought the English army to a decisive battle, and he (Buonaparte) had therefore been the more anxious to push on, and if possible force it, as he considered nothing else could offer him a chance of surmounting the difficulties with which he was surrounded : but, he added, if he could have beaten the English army, which (from the approximation of their numbers) he was led to consider possible, the situation was such that he was positive hardly any of the English forces would have escaped being either killed or taken ; that the Russian army, having been already beaten on the 16th, would (upon any decided disaster to the English) have been forced to make a precipitate retreat and perhaps have been dispersed, certainly entirely disorganized ; that he (Buonaparte) might then have pushed by forced marches to have met the Austrians before any junction could have taken place between them and the Russians, which would have placed the game in his hands even if hostilities had been obstinately persevered in ; though, in the then state of things, he had built, he said, rather upon the idea that a victory over the English army in Belgium, with its immediate results, would have been sufficient to have produced a change in the Administration in England

and have afforded him a chance of concluding an immediate general truce; which was really his first object, as France was hardly equal to the effort she was then making, and it was perfectly impossible for her to think of making any adequate resistance against the numerous forces of the Allies if once united and acting in concert against him.

He said things, however, having taken the turn they did, and forced him, consequently, to act as he had done, he thought Great Britain had not pursued the wisest policy in refusing to receive him in a friendly manner; that he would have given *his word of honour* not to have quitted the kingdom nor to have interfered in any manner, directly or indirectly, in the affairs of France or in politics of any sort, unless hereafter requested so to do by our Government; that the influence he had over the minds of people of every description in France would have enabled him to have kept them quiet under whatever terms it might have been thought necessary for the future security to impose upon France; but that if terms at all repugnant to the vanity of the French nation are acquiesced in by the Bourbons it will render them, if possible, even more unpopular than they now are, and the people of France will only await a favourable crisis to rise *en masse* for their destruction. He said the disbanding of the French Army was of no great consequence, as the whole nation was now military and could always form into an army at a given signal. In answer to all this I told him very fairly that, conscious as *he* no doubt was of *his* own integrity and how sacredly he would have observed any stipulations to which he pledged *his word of honour*, it was, perhaps, natural for him at the moment to feel as he had stated; yet that I did not think, after the events of latter years, the Government of Great Britain could be supposed to have sufficient reliance on him to have allowed him to take up his abode in England in conformity with his request, due reference being had to the present state of things in France and to the feelings of our allies on the Continent; and I therefore observed to him, that, with this view of the subject, I had been surprised at his not retiring in preference to Austria, where his connection with the Emperor would have afforded him so strong a claim to more distinguished reception and consideration. He said if he had gone there he had no doubt he would have been received with every attention, but that he could not bring himself to receive any favours from the Emperor of Austria after the manner in which he had now taken part against him, notwithstanding his former professions of affection and his close connection with him ; which latter, the General added, had not been by any means sought by himself. He then gave me the following curious relation respecting his marriage with Maria Louisa. He told me that when he was with the Emperor of Russia at Erfurth, Alexander took an opportunity of pressing upon him one day how important his having a legitimate heir must prove to the repose of France and Europe ; and Alexander therefore advised his setting aside Josephine, to which, if he would consent, the Emperor offered him in marriage a Russian princess (Buonaparte said he believed the Emperor called her the Princess Ann) ; but he said he did not pay much attention to it at the time, for he had lived so long in such harmony, and had so much reason to be satisfied, with Josephine, that the idea of causing her pain disinclined him from then entering further on the subject ; added to which, he said, he was already well aware of the falseness of character of the Emperor Alexander. He therefore merely observed to him in reply, that he was living on the best terms possible with the Empress Josephine, and consequently had never turned his thoughts towards any arrangement of the nature mentioned by his Imperial Majesty. However, some time afterwards at Paris, being strongly pressed by his friends on the same point, and Josephine having herself assented to the arrangement, he sent to Russia to acquaint Alexander with his wish and readiness to espouse the Russian princess who had been proffered to him. This intimation, he said, the Russian government received with every outward mark of satisfaction, professing its readiness to accede to the match, but at the same time starting difficulties upon various points connected with it, and particularly with regard to securing to the Princess the right of exercising her own religion, to which end it was demanded a Greek chapel might be established for her in the Tuilleries. This, Buonaparte said he would not have cared about himself, but being a thing so uncustomary, it, with the other points requested by Russia, caused much discussion and difficulty at Paris; therefore, in consequence of these

C

inconveniences presenting themselves with regard to the Russian alliance, some of his
ministers, with Eugene Beauharnois (his son-
in-law), waited upon him to press the advantage
it would be if he would consent to ask in
marriage an Austrian princess instead, adding
that the Austrian Ambassador would readily
engage for his court coming into any arrangements he (Buonaparte) might wish for this
object ; to which he replied if such were the
case, and the thing could be concluded at once,
he should not on his part make objections to
this new plan. It was, therefore, almost immediately agreed upon to take the contract of
marriage of Louis XVI. for their guide in
arranging his with an Austrian princess, and
before twelve o'clock that night the necessary
documents were prepared and signed and sent
off for the approbation of the Emperor of
Austria; who acceded without hesitation to
everything, and by his manner of forwarding
it, gave all reason to believe that he was not
only satisfied, but highly pleased with the
arrangement; and thus Buonaparte said he
became the Emperor's son-in-law without any
other solicitation or intrigue on his part, and
without having even once seen Maria Louisa

until she arrived in France as his wife. He therefore seemed to think that the Emperor's conduct towards him, since his reverses began, was not in unison with his conduct or professions towards him in prosperity, or such as he had a right to expect from the father of his wife; and consequently he said he would rather have gone anywhere in his distress, or done anything, than have placed himself in a situation to have been obliged to ask protection *as a favour* from a prince who he thought had behaved towards him so unjustly. He finished by saying he had been deceived with respect to the reception he looked for from the English, but still, harshly and unfairly as he considered himself treated by them, yet he found comfort from feeling that he was under the protection of British laws; which he could not have felt had he gone to any other country, where his fate might have depended on the whim of an individual. He hardly said anything more about his wish to have gone to America, and though his attendants assured me he was very anxious to have got there, and to have remained there as a private individual, I believe he gave up all idea of that country after the passports were refused him, and he saw the situation of our ships. He played his game of vingt-un this evening as usual, and went to bed about ten o'clock.

Our latitude and longitude were to-day at noon 42° 59' N., and 10° 42' W.

On the 17th August we had light baffling weather. In my conversation this day with General Buonaparte, the only thing which passed, worthy of noticing, was his remarking to me, amongst other things, that he had been placed in chief command as a General Officer at the age of twenty-four years; that he made the conquest of Italy at twenty-five; that he had risen from nothing to be sovereign of his country (as Consul) at thirty; and that if chance had caused him to have died or to have been killed the day after he entered Moscow, his would have been a career of advancement and uninterrupted success without a parallel; and the very misfortunes which afterwards befel the French Army would in such case probably have tended rather to the advantage than disadvantage of his fame, as, however inevitable they were, they would certainly have been attributed to *his* loss rather than to their true cause.

The General left the vingt-un party rather

abruptly this evening and retired earlier than usual.

Our latitude and longitude this day were 41° 57' N., 11° 11' W.

On the 18th *August* we had fine weather with light winds from the westward. The brig I sent to Guernsey joined us again this day, which enabled me to give General Buonaparte some French papers and gazettes which she brought. He told me in the evening that the Presidents des Departements and des Arrondissements appointed by the King were, with very few exceptions, the same persons as he (Buonaparte) should have appointed. In the course of our conversation this evening he talked much of the late Queen of Naples and said he had had a good deal of correspondence with her, as well whilst he was in Sicily as in Naples : he said his general advice to her was to remain quiet and not to intermeddle with the arrangements of the greater Powers of Europe. By letters which, he said, he had received from his wife, he learned that after the Queen of Naples had returned to Vienna she had taken notice of and been very kind to his son, and that in a conversation she had with his wife she had asked her why she did not follow him (Buonaparte) to Elba. Maria Louisa answered that she wished to do so, but her father and mother would not allow her, &c. The Queen of Naples then interrogated her as to whether she really liked him, when, being answered in the affirmative, and Maria Louisa speaking further in his favour, the Queen said to her, " My child, when one has the *happiness to be married to such a man*, papas and mammas should not keep one away from him whilst there are windows and sheets by which an escape to him might be effected." If there be any truth in the Archduchess having written to him in this style whilst he was at Elba, it will tend to prove that she entertained some idea of his restoration to power; for were she (as he would infer by it) really attached to him, she would, I think, have been more likely to have attempted following the Queen of Naples' advice than to have written about it.

In the course of this evening's conversation he told me that he considered the Russians and Poles to be decidedly a braver race of people than all the rest of Europe excepting the French and English, and in particular very superior to the Austrians. He said that the Emperor of Austria had neither abilities nor firmness of character; that the King of Prussia was *un pauvre bête* ; that the Emperor Alexander was a more active and clever man than any of the Sovereigns of Europe, but that he was extremely false ; and he asked me if I was aware that, when in friendship with him at Erfurth, he had signed with him a joint letter to the King of England to request His Majesty would relinquish the right of maritime visitation of Neutrals.

He said Russia was much to be feared if Poland was not preserved as an independent nation, to be a barrier between Russia (which was already able to call forth such hordes of soldiers) and the rest of Europe. He added, however, that whatever might be decided on this subject at the Congress, *he did not think* Russia would succeed in making Poland an appendage to the Empire, the Poles being too brave and too determined ever to be brought to submit quietly to what they considered as disgrace and national degradation. He spoke in high terms of the King of Saxony, and said he was the only sovereign who had kept faith with him to the last. He mentioned to me also that, after his arrival at Paris from Elba, he

had received assurances, both from the King
of Spain and from the Portuguese, that, whatever appearances they might be forced to make,
he might depend on their not taking any active
offensive part against him. He talked to me
of many of our principal characters in England, and stated particularly the high respect
he entertained for the character of the late
Lord Cornwallis, whose manners and behaviour at Amiens he spoke of as being most
noble and honourable, both to himself and his
country. He spoke in equal terms of panegyric
of Mr. Fox, with whom he said he had had
much conversation when he was in France.
He likewise talked of several other people in
England, but not in so flattering a strain as of
those I have mentioned. He told me he had
formed a great friendship with Captain Usher,
who conveyed him to Elba, and added that he
had hoped to have seen him at Paris; that he
had confidently looked for a visit from him
there, and was much disappointed at his not
coming to see him in his prosperity, as he had
commenced acquaintance with him in his ad-
versity.

He told me this evening, likewise, that he
had gained possession of a correspondence

from a foreign royal personage of. high consideration in England, which spoke very disrespectfully of different branches of our Royal Family; that he (Buonaparte) had been on the point of publishing these letters in *The Moniteur*, but had desisted, or rather recalled them from the publisher, at the earnest intercession of, and from consideration towards, the person by whose means he obtained them.

Our latitude and longitude to-day were 40° 50′ N., 11° 20′ W.

On the 19th *August*, our weather was moderate with a pleasant breeze from the N.W. General Buonaparte, since on board the " Northumberland," has kept nearly the same hours: he gets up late (between ten and eleven); he then has his breakfast (of meat and wine) in his bed-room, and continues there in his *déshabillé* until he dresses for dinner, generally between three and four in the afternoon; he then comes out of his bed cabin and either takes a short walk on deck or plays a game of chess with one of his Generals until the dinner hour (which is five o'clock). At dinner he generally eats and drinks a great deal and talks but little; he prefers meats of all kinds highly dressed and never touches vegetables. After dinner he generally walks for about an hour or hour and-a-half, and it is during these walks that I usually have the most free and pleasant conversations with him. About eight he quits the deck, and we then make up a game at cards for him, in which he seems to engage with considerable pleasure and interest until about ten, when he retires to his bed-room, and I believes goes almost immediately to bed. Such a life of inactivity, with the quantity and description of his food, makes me fear he will not retain his health through the voyage; he however as yet does not appear to suffer any inconvenience from it.

In our conversation this evening he gave me an amusing account of being admitted a Mussulman. When in Egypt he said the Sheiks and other Chiefs there had many consultations on the subject, but at last admitted him and his followers amongst the Faithful, and with express permission to drink wine, provided that every bottle they opened they would determine to do some good action. On his requiring an explanation of what was intended by the term a good action, the head Sheik informed him they meant such as giving charity to people in distress, making a well in a desert, building a mosque, and such like.

. He said, had he continued in Egypt, things would not have ended there as they did; that Kleber was an excellent man, and a good soldier, but that he did not understand or try to manage the people of the country, and that he had beaten one of the principal sheiks, which, being considered an indignity to the whole, caused him to be assassinated; and he said General Menon, who succeeded him, though a brave man, had no abilities whatever. He told me the Turks had sent two or three people at different times to kill him (Buonaparte); but that the people of the country, from his having humoured them and made friends with them, always gave him sufficient warning, and prevented the assassins getting near him; whereas, he said, the man who killed Kleber had been suffered to hide himself in Kleber's garden, and when the General was walking there alone, he sprang upon him unawares and stabbed him; after which, instead of attempting to escape, he sat down at one end of the garden until he was taken by the General's guard, almost immediately after he had perpetrated the deed.

If Buonaparte had any share in causing the death of Kleber (as has been generally reported), he certainly is the most consummate hypocrite that ever existed, for I eyed him closely whilst he was talking to me about it, and he certainly did not betray the least embarrassment or hesitation whilst telling his story.

In answer to a question I put to him, he said if everything had turned out in Egypt according to the best hopes and wishes he entertained when he sailed for that country, yet, that he should nevertheless have returned as he did in consequence of the information he received from France. He played at cards as usual this evening until about half-past ten, and he appeared in excellent humour and spirits.

Our latitude and longitude this day at noon were 39° 9' N. and 11° 26' W.

On the *20th August* the weather continued fine, and would have been pleasant but for the swell. Being Sunday, Divine Service was performed on board, and I was rather surprised that none of my French passengers attended, even from curiosity. I did not see the General to-day until dinner-time. At dinner he asked the clergyman many questions with respect to the differences between our religion and the Roman Catholic. After dinner he walked but a very short time, and then went directly to his sleeping cabin, which I attributed to his having observed the preceding Sunday that neither myself nor any of the officers of the ship joined in his card party, and his not choosing to risk infringing any of our regulations.

Our latitude and longitude to-day were 37° 19' N. and 12° 14' W.

On the 21st *August* our weather continued much the same, but rather more thick and cloudy, and the wind, though light, veering to the N.E. Captain Hamilton of the "Havannah," and Captain Mansell of the 53rd, dined with me to-day. Buonaparte was pleasant, and talked, more than usual, with them, but on indifferent subjects. Our dinner having been later than usual, curtailed our customary walk and conversation, and he went to his card party almost immediately after getting up from dinner. He played, however, only until about half-past nine, and then retired to his bed-room. His French friends generally continue playing after he retires, until about eleven. They do not breakfast with me in the morning at eight; but have one for themselves more according to their palates, of hot meats with wines, between ten and eleven, before which time (like their chief), they seldom get up.

Our latitude and longitude to-day at noon were 35° 56' N. and 13° 16' W.

On the *22nd August* we got the N.E. wind which usually prevails in these latitudes, with fine weather, though unpleasantly hazy. General Buonaparte requested me to write home from Madeira for some books for him, which I promised to do. All my French party have been engaged writing letters this day for Europe to send to Madeira as we pass it. Buonaparte asked me at dinner several questions about the different islands in the Atlantic; to what nations they belonged and so forth. His ignorance on these points seems quite wonderful, and I cannot understand what object he can have in pretending to be so if not so in reality.

He said to-day that had he continued at the head of the French Government in peace, and had found it to have been within his power, he never would have attempted the occupation of St. Domingo; that the most he would willingly have established with regard to that island would have been to have kept frigates and sloops stationed round it to force the blacks to receive everything they wanted from, and to export all their produce exclusively to, France; for, he added, he considered the independence of the blacks there to be more likely to prove detrimental to England than to France (and it really appears that in all his calculations he has made or does make, the proportion of evil which may accrue to England from any measure bears always in his mind the first consideration).

He complained to-day of suffering much from the heat: he played, however, at cards until ten o'clock and then went to his room.

Our latitude and longitude to-day were 34° 58' N. and 13° 31' W.

On the 23rd August our N.E. wind veered to E., freshened, and the weather became hot, hazy and unpleasant. Soon after noon we made the Island of Porto Santo and afterwards Madeira. General Buonaparte did not come on deck before dinner, as I expected he would have done, to look at the land, and during dinner he appeared thoughtful and out of spirits, as if the passing of this island made him reflect the more strongly on the little chance he had of ever seeing Europe again. He went upon deck, however, after dinner, and observed the island very particularly whilst we ran down along it, until we brought-to close off Funchal after dark, when he went into the cabin and played a game or two at piquet and then retired for the night to his bed-room, evidently not so well or not in such good spirits as on many of the preceding days.

We were this day at noon about nine leagues E.S.E. of Porto Santo.

On the 24*th August* we remained lying-to off the town of Funchal. I sent the frigate and troopships to the anchorage with my letters for England and to procure water and refreshments. We were unfortunate in having a very strong and unpleasant siroc wind which kept the thermometer above 80°. General Buonaparte came out of his cabin earlier than usual to look at and make his remarks on the town, which he had not been able to make out last night, and he appeared better than yesterday.

Mr. Veitch, His Majesty's Consul at Madeira, came on board, and I requested him to stay dinner. Buonaparte asked him a good many questions about the island, it's produce, it's height from the level of the sea, it's population, &c. He walked with Mr. Veitch and myself, talking on general topics, for about an hour after dinner, and then retired at once to his bed-room without joining the card table.

This day at noon we were off the town of Funchal, Madeira.

On the 25*th August* we had a continuance of the violent and disagreeable siroc wind. The frigate and troopships which had anchored in Funchal Roads did not rejoin me until about three o'clock, the strength of the wind having opposed great difficulties to them in procuring their water and other supplies; and after they did join, it occupied us until dark to remove the different things they brought out for those of the squadron which had remained under way; we then made sail again to the southward.

The heat of this day and the disagreeable nature of the wind, added to the motion of the ship, which was considerable, evidently affected General Buonaparte very much. He was on deck but little either before or after dinner; he seemed to have lost his appetite, and was in very low spirits and retired early to his bedroom. We were this day at noon about seven leagues S.W. of Madeira.

On the 26*th August*, though the wind continued from the E. its siroc qualities had quitted it (to our great relief) and this proved a pleasant cool day in comparison with what we had experienced off Madeira. The sea, which had been excited by the violence of the siroc wind, had likewise subsided, and with scarce any motion we ran about nine knots an hour during the day. This pleasant change brought General Buonaparte out of his bed-room early, and he appeared evidently better in health, though I observed at dinner he had not recovered his former appetite. After dinner he walked with me very late, talking generally of the affairs of Europe. He told me, amongst other things, that he had observed in some of the French papers brought from Guernsey, the King of Prussia was about to change the nature of his government, and to admit of national representation in it; he foretold that this would produce the greatest difficulties and mischief, both to the King of Prussia and Emperor of Austria; that he knew there were many revolutionary spirits in both those countries, and that the nations of the conti-nent were not adapted for a representative government like England. I remarked to him in reply that he had, however, admitted it into the constitutions which he had himself estab-lished in France. This he acknowledged, but added that he had not done so because he had considered it a wise measure for the nations, but because his situation at the moment required him to yield this point to the popular feeling; and it being, he said, at the time his particular interest to *substantiate* all the late innovations, and in short whatever differed essentially from the old system of government, thereby to render more difficult the restoration of the former order of things *and therewith the dynasty of the Bourbons.* He went again over the old ground of the military bias of the French nation, and the impolicy of exasperating the French people. He spoke much of their determined aversion to the Bourbons, which he said could not but be materially increased by the idea of that family being again put in possession of the government by means of foreign troops, who had carried ruin and devastation into the greatest part of the country; therefore he was quite sure the troubles in France were by no means at an end. They might, he said, be smothered for a moment by terror, and by the presence of the allied troops, but if these forces withdrew from the country whilst the recollection of events remained in the minds of the people, he averred that a general insurrection throughout France would immediately take place, and it would cost much difficulty and bloodshed ere it would again be suppressed.

He mentioned in the course of our conversation, that he had left his brother Jerome at Paris, who had determined to remain there in disguise for some time, and until he saw the turn affairs were likely to take; he added he did not know what befel him (Jerome) afterwards, as of course he had not been able to hear from him since.

After walking, and so conversing, in a frank strain until past nine o'clock, he went into the cabin and from thence almost immediately to his bedroom.

Our latitude and longitude this day at noon were 30° 53′ N., 17° 22′ W.

On the 27th *August*, we had a fine breeze from the N.E., but the weather became more than usually foggy and hazy, which I the more regretted as, General Buonaparte having expressed some curiosity respecting the Peak of Teneriffe and the Canary Islands, I caused the squadron to be this day steered between the Islands of Gomera and Palma for the purpose of gratifying his curiosity; but though we passed close to Gomera about mid-day, yet the haze continued so thick that we obtained but bad views of the land, and could only make it out very imperfectly and with much difficulty.

The General seemed much recovered to-day; he did not, however, walk before dinner, and our days are now so much shortened by having got so far to the southward that our walks and conversations after dinner are considerably curtailed. This evening he told me he had spent £3,000,000 sterling in the improvements at Cherbourg; that he had constructed a basin, or rather a kind of inner harbour (as it is without gates), which would contain thirty sail-of-the-line and which had fifty feet of depth at low water; that the outer road, which, he said, was now perfectly safe with all winds, would also contain thirty sail-of-the-line more; that he had arranged everything necessary for building ships there, and in short for making it a naval port of the first rank; and he added that he had conceived such an establishment, so situated, would have caused us much difficulty with reference to our possessions in Guernsey and Jersey. The only thing, he said, he had dreaded relative to it, and which he was taking therefore every precaution to avert, was our getting momentary possession of the place by a *coup de main* at any favourable juncture, and in which case he was aware that a few barrels of gunpowder, scientifically applied to the walls of his basins, cones, &c., might destroy in an instant what had cost so much time, expense, and labour to complete. He withdrew to his own cabin again very early this evening.

To-day at noon we were about four leagues W. from Gomera, with a fresh breeze from the N.E., running between the Islands at the rate of about eleven miles an hour.

On the 28*th August*, our N.E. trade continued, but not so fresh as yesterday, and the weather became hot, thermometer being from 78° to 80°. My French party appeared distant and much out of humour to-day, especially M. de Bertrand, who presumed to appear dissatisfied because I would not desire he might be permitted to have a light burning in his cabin throughout the night. I have, of course, left them to get out of this temper their own way, and have taken little or no notice of them throughout the day. General Buonaparte took but a short walk after dinner and I had very little conversation with him.

Our latitude and longitude this day at noon were 26° 2' N., 19° 9' W.

On the 29th *August*, we had a moderate trade wind with a good deal of swell. The day has passed nearly as the preceding one with regard to my passengers, and without any circumstance worthy of notice.

Our latitude and longitude this day at noon were 24° 23′ N., 20° 23′ W.

On the 30th *August*, we had a fresh trade wind, disagreeable weather and heavy swell, which made the ship roll much. Buonaparte seemed to suffer much from these causes, and though he attended our dinner party he ate very little, seemed disinclined to enter into conversation, and retired to his own room again soon after dinner.

Our latitude and longitude this day at noon were 22° 27′ N., and 22° 12′ W.

On the 31st *August*, the fresh trade wind and swell continued; the General, however, appeared better, though the rolling of the ship seemed still to affect him considerably. He mentioned to-day that, when his Army in Egypt was so severely visited by the plague, his soldiers, and indeed, the officers, became so disheartened that, as General-in-chief, he found it to be an absolutely necessary part of his duty to endeavour to give them confidence and reanimate

them by visiting frequently himself the plague
hospital, and talking to and cheering the
different patients in it. He said he caught
the disorder himself but recovered again
quickly; he added that those who kept up
their spirits, and did not give way to the idea
that they must die, generally recovered, but
those who desponded almost invariably died.
He played at chess with M. de Bertrand this
evening till later than his usual hour of going
to bed, and appeared in better spirits than for
two or three days past.

Our latitude and longitude to-day were
19° 53′ N., 25° 43′ W.

On the 1st *September*, we had a fresh trade
wind accompanied by uncommonly thick
weather, which prevented our making out
the Island of St. Antonio so soon as we expected; but, just as the sun set, we found
ourselves close to the S.W. end, not having
been able previously to discover any part of
it. I then brought-to with an intention of
communicating with the island in the morning,
and to wait for two brigs I had sent to reconnoitre the nearest shores to search for a convenient watering place.

Our conversation at table this day, and afterwards on deck, was principally with reference to the islands near us, and did not draw forth anything I have considered worth noticing.

General Buonaparte has given up his evening card parties for chess, at which game he has of late entertained himself from his dinner to his bed-time.

Our latitude and longitude to-day at noon were 17° 45' N., and 25° 4' W.

On the *2nd September*, about 1 a.m., the trade wind, which had been for some time strong, freshened to a perfect gale of wind, bringing with it a very heavy sea and violent rain. Soon after daylight the wind veered from N.E. to E., and then from E. to S.E. and S., still blowing hard, which rendered it impracticable for me to communicate with the islands; and the brigs I had sent to reconnoitre being driven off by the gale without effecting anything, I made the signal to put the crews of the squadron on short allowance of water, and pushed on again to the S.W. All my French passengers suffered much by the bad weather of the night; General Buonaparte, however, contrary to my expectation, made his appearance at dinner and seemed in tolerable spirits.

The weather moderated a little after dinner,

and this evening passed, with regard to the General, as the preceding one, without offering anything worthy of notice.

We were to-day at noon W.N.W. from the S.W. end of St. Antonio, about seven leagues distance; our latitude 17° 6' N.

On the *3rd September*, the wind continued from the S.E. and became light, baffling and calm at times, the weather extremely hot, the thermometer being from 82° to 83° throughout the day. General Buonaparte complained much of the heat, and I saw but little of him and had no conversation with him.

I took advantage of the calm to collect returns from the squadron, and had the satisfaction to find it unusually healthy; the troopships, with 448 persons on board the one, and 446 on board the other, having the one only *two*, and the other only *six*, in their respective weekly sick reports.

Our latitude and longitude this day were 16° 15' N., and 26° 30' W.

On the *4th September*, the calm weather which continued until a little after daylight was succeeded by a moderate breeze from the N.E., and though we had much swell from the S.W. the ship proceeded forward

on her course pleasantly, which brought
General Buonaparte from his cabin earlier
than usual. He was occupied playing at
chess before dinner, but after dinner I
had a long walk and a good deal of conversation with him, in the course of which
I was enabled to draw from him a relation
of the *Jaffa poisoning story*. His statement
of it was that, finding himself obliged
to evacuate Jaffa, and leave it to be taken
possession of by the troops of Djezzer Pacha
(whose cruelty of character was well known)
he ordered off before him all the sick and
wounded of the army that could be moved,
to facilitate which he lent even his own horses;
but the Chief Physician then represented to
him that there were a few Frenchmen in such
an advanced state of the plague that there did
not remain even a possibility of their recovery,
and that attempting to remove them with
the rest would endanger the whole army.
Knowing, however, as he (Buonaparte) well
did, that if these unhappy wretches fell into
the hands of Djezzer Pacha they would have
all sorts of cruelties practised on them in their
last moments, he felt the best thing he could
do was to order a council of all the medical

men in the army to be assembled, to ascertain,
in the first place, whether the removal of these
poor people, or any of them, might be effected
without endangering, in an unwarrantable
degree, the remainder of the army, and whether
there existed any chance of adequate benefit
accruing to themselves if their removal were
attempted; and, in the next place, if the council
agreed with the Chief Physician and confirmed
the absolute necessity of some being left
behind, then to consider whether it would not
be better for the individuals themselves to
accelerate their death by opium rather than leave
them in the state they were, to be tormented
by the implacable enemies into whose hands
they would inevitably be doomed to fall. He
said the council was public and everybody
knew what passed in it, and therefore he had
been surprised at the many contradictory
stories which he knew had gone abroad
respecting this transaction. He added that
after the medical council had finished its
deliberations, they reported to him it was
their decided opinion the people ought not,
on any account, to be removed, yet that the
majority of the council could not bear the idea
of adopting such a measure as accelerating the

death of individuals under their charge, however desperate their situations ; but they further stated they had every reason to believe all difficulties on this head would be done away, by the natural consequences of the disease under which these poor fellows laboured, if the General would so arrange as to retain the place forty-eight hours longer, at the expiration of which time they considered it scarcely possible that one of them could remain alive. Upon this report, the General told me, he immediately determined on retaining Jaffa the time specified by the board, and he continued in it himself, with the whole army, twenty-four hours longer, and then left a strong rear-guard to hold it the other twenty-four hours ; at the expiration of which, he said, the prediction of the medical officers was pretty well fulfilled by the death of almost every one of the patients in question, though, he added, he believed one or two might have been left not quite dead.* He considered the measure

---

* This part of the statement has since been confirmed to me by Captain Beattie, of the Marines, serving on board the "Northumberland," who belonged to the "Theseus" in Egypt, and entered Jaffa immediately after the French quitted it, and even before the troops of Djezzer Pacha ; he assures me there were only three or four Frenchmen found alive, and those in an advanced stage of the plague.

he wished to have adopted as more worthy of praise than of censure, and said had he been one of the people afflicted he should have considered it the greatest act of kindness to have been so dealt with, rather than left (without hope of recovery) to be tormented by such wanton savages as Djezzer Pacha's troops. Thus by his own acknowledgment (at least as far as regards his ideas and orders thereupon) is now placed beyond doubt a circumstance, which, from its nature and the numbers who have constantly denied it, has not been hitherto generally credited, and which has been also, very recently, flatly contradicted in a publication stated to have been written by a person who never quitted him for fifteen years.

In the course of this evening's conversation, Buonaparte also mentioned to me particulars of what passed between the Queen of Prussia and himself at Tilsit, when (to solicit that Magdeburg might be left to Prussia) she joined the royal party already assembled there. He said that had she arrived there sooner, it was probable she would have gained her point in this particular, not only by reason of the great advantage an extremely clever and fine woman

of high rank must always have when *personally*
urging any suit she has much at heart, but also
from the inclination he (Buonaparte) then had
to meet (as far as he conveniently could) the
wishes of the Emperor Alexander, who he
did not hesitate in affirming was at the time a
strongly attached *and much favoured* admirer of
her Prussian Majesty. It was, he said, owing
to the King of Prussia being apprised of this
latter circumstance, and consequently being
extremely jealous of the Emperor of Russia,
that the former prevented the Queen from
coming sooner to Tilsit, and until the Prussian
ministers, towards the closing of the arrangements, urged him in the strongest manner to
send for her, that they might have the benefit
of her abilities and influence to second their
endeavours to obtain better terms for Prussia ;
to which at length the King consenting, she
arrived accordingly, and the whole party being
to dine with him (General Buonaparte), she
was introduced to him before dinner, and
entered with great vivacity and ability upon
the subject of the approaching treaty, and
strongly solicited, as a personal favour to herself, that he would consent to leave Magdeburg
to Prussia, which, she said, would bind her

family to him by the strongest ties of gratitude, as well as respect. The General said Her Majesty pressed her suit warmly and cleverly; but he merely replied to all she said in general terms of civility, and avoided giving her any decided answer, or entering at all with her into the merits of the question; notwithstanding, it was evident by her behaviour at dinner that she entertained sanguine hopes of succeeding. He said she sat between the Emperor of Russia and himself, and although most elegant and amiable in her manners, she did not for a moment forget the object she had in view; and in proof of this, he added that at the dessert (I think he said), or in the evening, on his offering her a rose* he took out of a vase near him, she, on taking it, asked him immediately if she might consider it as a token of friendship, and of his having acceded to her request. Being, however, he said, upon his guard, and resolved not to be thus caught by surprise, he parried the attack with some general remarks

---

*I have noted particularly what the General told me respecting this rose, and his conversation at the time with the Queen of Prussia, as the author of the book "stated to be written by a person who never quitted him for fifteen years" mentions this circumstance, but states it very differently.

respecting the light in which alone civilities of this description should be regarded, and then turned the conversation. Notwithstanding this, however, and his having been extremely cautious throughout the evening not to allow anything to escape him which might in the slightest degree authorise the Queen to believe him inclined to yield to her solicitation, yet when she went away she appeared to be well satisfied, and to have persuaded herself that her endeavours were not to prove unsuccessful. The General said that therefore, thinking it would be impolitic to leave the question any longer open to discussion, he caused the Treaty to be signed at once on the next morning, and, of course, without any alterations in it in favour of Prussia. When the Queen came the next day to dinner, he said she showed evidently by her manner that she was piqued and much hurt, but she behaved with great dignity, and did not once allude to the Treaty, nor to anything which had passed respecting it, until going away in the evening, when, as General Buonaparte was handing her to her carriage, she mentioned to him how much he had disappointed her by the refusal of her request: that, had he complied, it would have attached her whole family to him for ever, and so forth ; to which he only answered that he should ever consider it one of the greatest misfortunes of his life that it had not been within his power to obey her Majesty's commands in this affair, begging her, however, to believe it would always afford him the highest gratification to be able to meet any wish of her's, and adding more civil speeches of this kind ; (" *mais* " said he to me, with a self-applauding smile, " *tout cela n'etoit pas Magdebourg*,") and having reached her carriage he put her into it, bade her good night, and left her. He added that previous, however, to her driving off, she sent for Duroc (the Grand Maréchal of his Palace) to her carriage, when, giving vent to her feelings, which she had till then so well stifled, she could not refrain from tears whilst she complained to him of the great disappointment, and told him how much she had been deceived in Buonaparte's character, and hurt by what had passed, &c., and early the next morning he said he received a message from her to say that, being taken suddenly ill, she had been forced to quit Tilsit and return home ; and thus, he added, Magdeburg was retained, though perhaps he had suffered somewhat by it in the good graces of her Prussian Majesty. He told me he thought her a most elegant engaging woman, and as handsome as could be expected in a woman thirty-five years of age. He spoke, however, very badly of her character as a wife, and particularly with reference to the Emperor Alexander; to oblige whom, he mentioned *(as a good joke)*, that he detained the King of Prussia a whole day by announcing an intention of paying him a formal visit, of which the Emperor Alexander took a premeditated advantage by setting off to obtain thereby an uninterrupted *tête-à-tête* visit with the Queen!!!

Having walked with me recounting these stories till later than usual, he did not make his appearance in the great cabin but retired to his own room at once.

Our latitude and longitude this day at noon were 15° 34′ N. and 26° 36′ W.

On the *5th September* we had a moderate trade wind but excessively hot weather, and nothing occurred during the day with regard to General Buonaparte worthy of notice. Our latitude and longitude at noon was 13° 58′ N. and 25° 30′ W.

On the *6th September* our trade wind continued till about four in the evening, when we experi-

enced excessively heavy rain, and the wind
gradually died away until it failed us altogether
and was succeeded by a southerly wind. To
my great surprise, after General Buonaparte had
eaten his dinner he got up to take his walk as
usual, and upon my remarking to him that it
was still pouring with rain, and therefore
advising him not to go out in it, he treated it
lightly and said it would not hurt him more
than the sailors he observed at the time
catching water, working and running about in
it. Of course I no longer opposed his whim,
and out he went in the rain accompanied by
two of his French friends, who, though obliged
to attend him, seemed by no means to enjoy
the idea of the wetting they were doomed to
get *par complaisance*. I have no doubt General
Buonaparte intended this dash of his should
give us a great idea of his hardiness of
character ; as, however, no further particular
notice was taken of it by any of us, and finding
it, I suppose, more unpleasant than he expected,
his walk was of very short duration, and being,
as was inevitable, perfectly wet through, he,
immediately on quitting the deck, went into
his own cabin, from whence he did not rejoin
us during the evening.

Our latitude and longitude this day at noon were 12° 41' N. and 23° 55' W.

From the 6th to this day, the 23rd September (on which we crossed the Equator about the meridian of Greenwich), General Buonaparte, continuing to keep nearly the same hours, and to follow the same routine of eating, drinking and sleeping, as before noticed, and my usual conversations with him after dinner having suffered considerable interruption from the shortness of the evenings and from his own people keeping more closely about him during his evening walks than formerly, so little variety of matter has offered for detailing on each successive day that I have been induced to combine this period; throughout the most of which we have experienced moderate S.S.W. winds with cloudy weather, accompanied occasionally with rain, and the air from these causes has been more cool and pleasant than we expected to meet with in such latitudes.

In the course of the different short conversations I managed to have with the General in this interval, he told me that had he succeeded in his attempt against England and reached *London*, his chief object and first endeavour would have been to have *there* concluded a

peace, which he should have immediately offered
on moderate terms ; but what, under such
circumstances, he would have considered moderate terms I could not draw from him (nor did
I think it very material), but the relinquishment
of the right of maritime visitation of neutrality
was one of the points he certainly would have
insisted upon. In another conversation on the
subject of the Russian expedition, he assured
me in the strongest manner that the only object
he had when he undertook it, and all he should
have asked had he been successful, was the
Independence of Poland (to which nation he
intended leaving the free choice of their own
king, only recommending Poniatowsky to them
as worthy of such distinction), and to make the
Emperor of Russia engage to join firmly in the
continental system against commercial inter-
course of any sort with England until its
Government should be brought to agree to
what he termed " the Independence of the
Seas." He, however, when subsequently talking to me of Moscow, let out that he had
procured there numerous emissaries to disperse
throughout the country amongst the Russian
peasantry to bias them in *his* favour and against
their own Government; to explain to them the

miseries they suffered from the unjust state of slavery in which they were kept; and to offer them freedom and protection if they would seek it through his means. He said he had at the time already received applications from different bodies of them, and had he been able to have maintained himself in the country he was quite sure he should have had the mass of the population in his favour. He told me that, prior to the death of the Emperor Paul, he (Buonaparte), whilst he was First Consul, had received seven or eight letters, written in his Imperial Majesty's own hand, pressing him to enter into close and intimate alliance with Russia, for the express purpose of exerting the united efforts of the two countries to humble Great Britain; and the Emperor proposed (if Buonaparte approved of it) to send off at once a large Russian army to act against the English interests in India. The General said he was about to dispatch a confidential ambassador with full powers to make the necessary arrangements, and to communicate to the Emperor his sentiments on these points, when he received the unwelcome intelligence of the Emperor's assassination. He added that, from the opinion the Emperor Paul seemed by his letters to entertain of him (the General), and from the great confidence he appeared to place in him, he had no doubt, if their negotiation had gone on, he would shortly have attained sufficient ascendancy with the Emperor to have induced him to change the foolish and impolitic course he was then pursuing in his own country; in which case his life would probably have been saved, and he might have become an ally of great importance to the French, and therefore the General said he considered Paul's death at the moment as a particularly untoward circumstance.

In a conversation on the propriety of the different capitals of Europe being sufficiently fortified to enable them to withstand for a short time a sudden advance and attack of an enemy's army, he told me he had long foreseen the propriety of having works of this kind around Paris, but he had been restrained from ordering them by his dread of the effect it might have on the public opinion, in concert with which he had considered it a requisite policy always to act, and which, even in the zenith of his power, he had never felt himself strong enough to disregard; and, he added, he knew full well the French character to be such that until danger was at their gates they could not have borne the idea of such a precaution being for a moment necessary.

Speaking again on the subject of his meditated invasion of England, I asked him if he had procured any plans of our fortifications at Chatham. He told me he had not, but that he had a general idea of the lines there, and that he had had no doubt of procuring in time such further information on the subject as was necessary for him. He said he had got his intelligence very regularly from England by means of our smuggling boats, and that amongst others *Mr. Goldsmith* (the Editor) had conveyed to him much useful information. He told me he had had a personal interview with him at Boulogne at one of the periods he (Goldsmith) came over in one of these smuggling boats, and he said considerable sums had been paid him by the police office at different times for services of this nature. I mention this because I have determined to note down herein every particular this extraordinary man tells; but it is right I should at the same time remark that there was a something of malicious cunning in General Buonaparte's manner whilst making this statement which induced me very much to doubt the truth of the whole story; and I was rather inclined to think he made this assertion (which was in public, at my table) either with a view to make us fancy all Mr. Goldsmith had written against him was merely as a cloak to cover his (Goldsmith's) own treasons, or (which is perhaps more probable) he hoped by such a statement so made, and therefore likely to be repeated, that he might cause public suspicion to fall on Mr. Goldsmith, which might perhaps draw him into difficulties, and thereby offer General Buonaparte some chance of being revenged upon him for the unqualified abuse he has so lavishly heaped upon the General and his family. He further observed that he believed Mr. Goldsmith was possessed of some talent, although a consummate rogue, and he then immediately turned the conversation to other matter.

On another day, talking of Ireland, he told me he had arranged everything with that country, and if he could have got safely over to it the force he intended sending, the party there in his favour was so strong that he had every reason to suppose they would have succeeded in possessing themselves of the whole Island. He said he had held constant communication with the disaffected party, which he averred was by no means confined to the Roman Catholics, but had also a very large proportion of Protestants. He of course did not give me any of their names, nor did I think it right to ask him for them. He said he always acquiesced in everything they asked for, leaving all arrangements respecting the Country, Religion, &c., entirely to themselves; his grand and only object being to gain the advantageous point, for him, of separating Ireland from England on *any* terms, and to have it on his side in opposition to England. He told me those who came to him from Ireland generally came and returned through London, by which means he obtained information from them respecting both countries; and they crossed the Channel backwards and forwards with little risk or difficulty by the means likewise of his friends the smugglers; but he said, notwithstanding the great advantages he thus derived from these smugglers, he found out at last that they played a similar game backwards and forwards, and carried us as much intelligence to England as they brought him from it, and he was therefore obliged to forbid their being any longer admitted at Dunkirk, or indeed anywhere but at *Gravelines*; where he established particular regulations respecting them, and did not allow them to pass a barrier which he caused to be fixed for the purpose, and where he placed a guard to watch them, and to prevent their having unnecessary communication with the country; and he ordered the goods and other articles they wished to have to be brought down for them to this barrier, for which they paid a small additional impost.

Soon after we had crossed the Equator to-day, the Comte de Bertrand came to me from General Buonaparte to say that, it being a general custom of all nations for those who had not passed the Equator to submit to certain ceremonies, or to pay for exemption some trifling tribute to those who had crossed it, he (the General) wished, if I had no objection to it, to send our seamen, who were at the time going through the usual process, *one or two hundred* napoleons. As I considered this to be an attempt of the General's to avail himself, with his usual *finesse*, of a plausible excuse to distribute such a large sum amongst the seamen, solely with a view of rendering himself popular with them, I, of course, not only refused my assent to this request, but pointedly prohibited it. I told him the custom of the ships of our nation was, for those whose rank and station authorized them to look for indulgence on these occasions, usually to send a bottle of rum to the seamen; but this being incompatible with the discipline of a man-of-war, officers of the " Northumberland" who had not crossed the line, had given, in lieu of rum, the subordinate officers one dollar, and the higher officers half-a-guinea each, and if General Buonaparte felt extremely anxious to give something more, I would, though reluctantly, say he might give as far as five napoleons ; but that that sum was the utmost I could allow of under existing circumstances. The Grand Maréchal, in reply, endeavoured to persuade me that what General Buonaparte should give on such an occasion ought not to be weighed by what was given by officers of the profession, and that the sum of one hundred napoleons was the least which such a person could offer on so extraordinary an occasion as his crossing the Equator. His rhetoric, however, as usual, not having the slightest effect towards changing my determination, he was forced to return back to his master with my answer, who very wisely let the matter then drop, and did not say anything further on the subject, nor did he by his manner at dinner show that he was hurt or piqued by the refusal. I understand, however, he did *not* send the *five* napoleons for which I granted permission.

It is worthy of remark that this day we have passed *zero* of latitude and zero of longitude, and the sun the zero of its declination.

From the *23rd September* to this day, the *6th October* (which period, like the preceding, I combine to avoid uninteresting monotonous details), we have had the wind with little or no variation from S.W., accompanied with a heavy swell from the westward, the weather being cloudy and very cool, almost indeed amounting to cold, but without rain. By continuing pertinaciously on the starboard tack for the purpose of gaining all the southing possible, in the hope of thereby meeting sooner the S.E. trade-wind, we have got as near as within 30 leagues of the coast, in latitude 9° 36', but the wind having to-day veered somewhat more to the southward has at last enabled me to put the ship's head to the westward with some prospect of advantage, and gives me reason to hope our distance from St. Helena will now be quickly diminished, which indeed is not less anxiously desired by myself than by my passengers, as restless Frenchmen with a foul wind make but unpleasant messmates. They have, however, continued better in health than could be reasonably expected considering the changes of climate they have gone through, the length of time since their first embarkation in the " Bellerophon," and the inactive life they have led in comparison with that to which they have been accustomed. Of the whole party Madame de Bertrand only has experienced a few days' confinement from a feverish attack, which, however, yielded almost immediately to bleeding, and amongst all the rest there has not been a complaint beyond a cold or sore throat of trifling nature and short continuance. General Buonaparte himself is certainly fatter and looking better than when he first came on board the " Northumberland," and I must say he has throughout shown far less impatience about the wind or the weather, and made less difficulties, than any of the rest of the party. Subsequently to the 23rd ultimo, in our conversations, he has mentioned to me that he caused, a short time back, a survey to be taken throughout France of the grown oak timber it contained fit for ship building, the report

made to him upon which stated that there
was actually sufficient quantity for building a
thousand sail of the line; but, he said, France
failed altogether in trees fit for masts, and those
they were therefore obliged to get from the
Baltic; but he having understood that the
Corsican firs were strong and tough enough
to serve for masts during the two years immediately after they were cut down (after which
only they lost their elasticity and became brittle),
and as nine of them could be brought to
France at as little expense as one from the
Baltic, he had latterly endeavoured to bring
the Corsican spars into use in the French navy,
authorising their being sawn up for plank or
other use after having served as topmasts for
two years. But this plan, he said, did not
appear to be much approved of by the people
of the Marine Department, as there existed
extraordinary prejudice throughout the French
Navy against masts made from any spars
except those brought from the Baltic. He
told me there was a large quantity of masts
belonging to the French Government at Copen-
hagen when Lord Nelson made the attack and
consequent convention there; that he (the
General) had been therefore, at the time,

alarmed for the safety of his spars, but the Danes kept their faith with him and he afterwards got them all safe to France. Some of them, he said, he was obliged to have brought almost the whole way by inland navigation, being much in want of them, and the coast being too closely watched by our cruisers to allow of his trusting them round by sea.

Speaking of the present navy of France, he told me some of the superior officers were tolerably good seamen, he believed, but none of them were good officers ; that the best of them had been taken during the Revolution from the India and other merchant service, and, the French Navy having been so little employed, they were quite unaccustomed to command in any very difficult or trying circumstances ; therefore, that when they had accidentally fallen into such situations, they always appeared to have lost their heads, and become quite confused, and that whatever they did was generally precisely what they ought not. He said Admiral Gantheaume did very well while with him (the General) at his elbow when they were coming from Egypt ; but, he added, if Admiral Gantheaume had been left to himself he would have been taken twenty times

F

over, for he was constantly wanting to change
the ship's course to avoid one enemy or another,
and would have, by such over-precautions,
lost as much by night as he gained by day.
He therefore, he said, obliged the Admiral
always to explain to him upon paper the exact
situation of the ship and the apprehended
danger, after which it almost always occurred
that he took upon himself to desire the Admiral
to continue on a straight course for Fréjus; and
to this alone he attributed their having got safe
in, as the Admiral's anxiety would certainly
have induced him to have acted very differently
had not he (the General) so interfered with
him, and thus left it to the Admiral only to exert
his seamanship to press the ships forward. He
told me also it was a curious fact that Admiral
Bruix, on their way up to Alexandria, had
actually explained to him very minutely the
decided disadvantage a fleet must labour under
by receiving at anchor an attack from an hostile
fleet under sail; and yet, from want of recollection and presence of mind upon emergencies,
which the General had alluded to, this Admiral,
a few weeks afterwards, received at anchor
Lord Nelson's attack, losing his own life and
nearly his whole fleet to exemplify the correct-

ness of his ideas and the impropriety of his conduct ; but which General Buonaparte said he was positive would not have happened (at least inasmuch as relates to the fighting at anchor) had he, the General, been on the spot. He added, on the same subject, that it struck him the French Admirals had generally, upon coming to action, lost too much time and been too anxious about forming lines and making manœuvres which had ultimately proved of no adequate advantage ; he had therefore desired they might be instructed that, for the future, on approaching an enemy, a signal to form a line, as convenient for mutual support, and afterwards a signal to engage, would always be deemed fully sufficient to make to those under their orders ; and after this the captain of every ship of the fleet was to be held individually responsible to the Government for getting the ship he commanded quickly into close battle, and doing his best towards the destruction of some one of the enemy ; which would at all events prevent the captains from covering their own neglect (as Dumanois had done) by attributing errors to their chief. He had, however, he said, latterly resolved (unless some extraordinary emergency made it necessary) *not* to venture any more line-of-battle ships to sea until he should have had it in his power to have sent from his different ports at once 120 sail of the line, for the making up of which number, he said, he had laid all his plans; and he affirmed that, from the efforts he intended to have made for the object, he believed very much time would not have elapsed before he would have completed them. In the meantime, he said, whatever it might have cost him, he had determined on always keeping ten sail of French frigates at sea for the purpose of making and improving his officers. He added that when his frigates had been sent on distant cruises they were apt to consider their danger pretty well over when once safely through our line of cruisers on the French coast, after which they generally relaxed their vigilance and precautions. He had, therefore, decided to order these ten frigates for the future to cruise only in the neighbourhood of England or Ireland, where they would be certain to have enemies, bad weather and dangerous coasts, to keep them always on the alert; and those who managed to escape being wrecked or captured must, of course, do much more mischief to our commerce than had ever been done by the French frigates heretofore sent into the open seas and southern latitudes! To the commanders of all those, he said, who returned safe from such service, he should have given great promotion and rewards, and as fast as he heard of any being taken or lost he should have supplied their places with fresh ones. On my remarking to him the difficulty I conceived he would have found in obtaining seamen to have followed up this plan, he told me, by the system of conscription for the marine, which he had lately established in all the maritime counties of France, he would have had as many seamen as he pleased. Its customary production, without any vexation, would have given him 20,000 men a year; and, he added that, already, for want of ships to put these seamen in, he had been obliged to form them into regiments for the protection of the coast. (These men, however, it must be observed herefrom, would only have been seamen because he chose to have them designated as such; not from any claim of having been to sea or of having served on shipboard, but merely because they had been born and raised in a maritime county).

In a conversation respecting the late campaigns, he told me that at the Battle of Wagram he had had under his command, *actually engaged* in the field, a greater number of men than in any of his other battles; they amounted, he said, to about 180,000, and that he had had at the same time in the field 1,000 pieces of cannon. At Moscow, he said, though not much short of the same number, yet he certainly had not quite so many; and at Leipsic he did not think that he had more than 140,000. In answer to a question I put to him, he told me he considered a General Clausel to be decidedly the most able military officer now in France. Maréchal Soult and others of the maréchals were, he said, brave and able men for carrying into execution operations previously planned; but to plan and execute with large armies, in his opinion, none of them were by any means equal to this General Clausel.

The troopships having fallen considerably to leeward to-day, I have determined not to wait any longer for them; being now so far on the voyage they must, at all events, get to St. Helena a day or two after me.

From the *6th October* the wind, remaining from S.S.W. to S., allowed us to continue on the larboard tack without losing ground to the northward, until we got at last the S.E. Trade on the 11th inst., having, however, previously passed the thirteenth degree S. latitude; and even then the Trade hung considerably to the southward, but the ship being so much to windward this became immaterial to us, and with a fine, strong, fair wind we made between two and three hundred miles a day until we reached St. Helena this morning (the 15th), the sixty-sixth day since we quitted the Lizard.

During the latter part of the voyage, General Buonaparte, speaking to me of himself, told me that it was the want of officers at the beginning of the Revolutionary War which caused him to be sent for (though then a very young Captain of Artillery) from the Northern Frontier, where he was serving, to take the command of the Artillery before Toulon; that almost immediately after his arrival at this station he had pointed out to General Corteaux the necessity of making a great effort to get possession of the place which was called Fort Mulgrave by us, which Buonaparte engaged to succeed in doing if General Corteaux would allow him, and foretold that that place, once taken, would oblige the English, immediately afterwards, to entirely evacuate Toulon. This proposal, however, General Corteaux would not listen to, and they therefore went on some time longer according to their former plans of attack without materially advancing in the siege or doing any real good, until, one of the Representatives of the People coming to the army to overlook what they were about (as was customary in those days), Buonaparte directly laid before him his plans, and, obtaining his approval, Corteaux was overruled and obliged to adopt the measures which Buonaparte had before proposed to him; which succeeding precisely according to his prediction, he was in reward immediately promoted to the rank of General of Brigade. He afterwards went with part of the same army into Savoy, where he rendered some further services; but it having been just then determined, in consequence of a scarcity of officers for the Infantry, to draft into it some of the officers of the Artillery, and it falling to his (General Buonaparte's) lot to be one of these, he quitted the army and went to Paris to remonstrate, and to endeavour to avoid being so exchanged; but meeting with an unfavourable reception from a General of Artillery, who was a Representative of the People and had

the chief management of these arrangements,
after some high words passing between them
he (Buonaparte) retired in disgust, and putting
on the dress of the Institute of Paris, to which
he then belonged (having been elected into it
in consequence of his proficiency in mathe-
matics), he continued in Paris endeavouring to
keep quiet and from the armies; which, he said,
however, he should have been obliged to have
joined (perhaps in a subordinate capacity), had
not the advance of the Austrian General,
De Vins, into Italy, and the retreat and alarm
of the French Army opposed to him, spread
considerable consternation in Paris; which
induced the Committee of Public Safety (that
knew General Buonaparte was well acquainted
with the geography of that country) to send for
him to consult with him on the best measures
to be adopted; and they were so satisfied with
what he laid before them on the subject that
they immediately caused him to draw up
instructions for their General in Italy founded
upon his (Buonaparte's) advice; and the Committee then directed that General Buonaparte
might remain near them at Paris to assist
them on such military points as they might
wish to consult him upon. The advice he

gave, as above mentioned, proved efficacious;
their Italian Army took up the position he had
pointed out, and thereby was enabled to stand
its ground without falling any further back,
in spite of every effort of the Austrian General
to force it, until it became strong enough to
attack in its turn; which it ultimately did, and
then (as is well known) defeated De Vins, and
was completely successful. Considerable credit
accrued to General Buonaparte on this account,
and he remained at Paris attached to the
Committee of Public Safety until the 13th
Vendemaire, the day on which the Convention
was attacked by the revolted sections of Paris;
which last having gained considerable advantages over the troops of the Convention, then
under the command of General Menon, Buonaparte was sent for by the Convention and
placed in command of the troops, in lieu of
General Menon; and he (Buonaparte) soon
succeeding in defeating the people of the section
and in restoring order, was as a reward immediately made Commandant of Paris; which
situation, he said, gave him considerable consequence and in which he continued until he
was made Commander-in-chief of the Army of
Italy. But he told me it was not until the

Battle of Lodi that any idea of his rising sufficiently in consequence to authorise his some day interfering in the Government of France, entered his imagination; but *then*, finding all his plans succeed so beyond even his own expectations, he began to look forward, though without any decided plan, to such events as afterwards took place; and he said the quantity of money which he sent from Italy to France, with these views, increased very considerably his popularity; but after his campaign of Italy and the consequent suspension of hostilities with Austria, he said the Directory became very jealous of him and were therefore anxious to get him into a scrape, to avoid which required his utmost caution and *finesse*, and induced him to refuse an appointment which had been offered to him to conduct the diplomatic discussions then going on with Austria, as also soon afterwards an appointment offered to him to command an Army for the invasion of England; but when the command of an expedition to Egypt was proposed to him, he immediately saw the advantage it offered him for getting out of the way of a jealous arbitrary Government, by its measures running itself to ruin, and by placing him at

the head of an army for an expedition almost
certain to be successful, leaving it open to
him to return with increased popularity when-
ever he might judge the crisis favourable ; therefore, he said, the Directory being anxious to
get him out of France and he being equally
anxious to get away from them, the Egyptian
Expedition did not fail to please both parties, and
he warmly entered into it the moment it was proposed ; but he assured me that the proposition
did not originate with himself, as has been
generally supposed. He said, having left
France with these ideas, he was anxiously
looking for the events which brought him back
even before they happened ; and on his return
to France he was soon well assured that there
no longer existed in it a party strong enough
to oppose him. He, therefore, immediately
planned the Revolution of the 18th Brumaire,
and though he might, he said, on that day
have run some little personal risk owing to
the general confusion, yet everything was so
arranged that it could not possibly have failed,
and the Government of France from that day
became inevitably and irretrievably in his
hands and those of his adherents ; and therefore, he said, all the stories I might have heard

of intentions of arresting him about that time,
and of opposing his intentions, were all non-
sense and without foundation in truth, for his
plans had been too long and too well laid to
admit of being so counteracted. After he became First Consul he said plots and conspiracies
against his life had, however, been very frequent, but by vigilance and some good fortune
they had all been discovered and frustrated.
He told me the one nearest proving fatal to him
was that in which Pichegru and Georges (and, he
added, Moreau) were concerned. He said thirty-
six of this party had been actually in Paris six
weeks, without the police knowing anything
of it; which was at last discovered by means
of an emigrant apothecary who, being informed against and secured after landing from
an English man-of-war (and the police having
entertained some suspicions in consequence of
the numbers that had been reported to have
been clandestinely landed about the same
time), it was judged would be a likely person
to bring to confession if properly managed;
therefore, being condemned to death and
every preparation made for his execution,
his life was offered him if he could give
any intelligence sufficiently important to

merit such indulgence; when he immediately
caught at the offer and gave the names of
the thirty-six persons before mentioned, every
one of whom, with Pichegru and Georges,
were (by the vigorous measures immediately
adopted) found and secured in Paris within a
fortnight. He said that, previous to this plot
being discovered, it would probably have proved
fatal to him, had not Georges insisted upon being
appointed a consul, which Moreau and Pichegru
would not hear of, and therefore Georges and
his party could not be brought to act. He told
me also that it was to be at hand for the purpose of aiding in these conspiracies, and to
take advantage of any confusion they might
create, that the Duc D'Enghien took up his
residence in the neighbourhood of Strasburg,
in which town he (Buonaparte) maintained
that he had certain information of the Duke
having been in disguise several times. On my
asking him if a report I had heard was true of
his having sent an order for the Duke's reprieve,
but which, unfortunately, arrived too late, he
told me it certainly was *not* true; that the Duke
was condemned for having conspired against
France, and he (Buonaparte) was determined
from the first to let the law take its course

respecting him, to endeavour if possible to check these frequent conspiracies. And in answer to my remonstrating against his having taken the Duke from the territories of the Duke of Baden, he said this did not, in his opinion, at all alter the case between France and the Duc D'Enghien; that the Duke of Baden might certainly have had some reason to complain of the violation of his territory, but that was an affair for him to settle with the Duke of Baden and not with the Duc D'Enghien; whom when they had got within the territory of France (no matter how), they had full right to try and punish for any act against the existing Government committed by him in France.

Thus does this man reason, who now exclaims so violently against the legality of our conduct in refusing to receive him in England, and sending him to reside at St. Helena.

22nd October.—Since General Buonaparte's arrival at St. Helena I have been so occupied that I have seen but little of him. I went with him, however, one day to *Longwood*, and he seemed tolerably satisfied with it, though with his attendants he has since been complaining a good deal; and having stated to me that he could not bear the crowds which gathered to see him in the town, he has, at his own request, been permitted to take up his residence (until Longwood should be completed) at a small house called the Briars, where there is a pretty good garden, and a tolerably large room, detached from the house, of which he has taken possession, and in which and the garden he remains almost all day; but in the evenings I understand he has regularly invited himself to join the family party in the house, where he plays at whist with the ladies of the family for sugar-plums until his usual hour of retiring for the night.

F I N I S .

Printed by the Army & Navy Co-operative Society, Limited, Westminster, S.W.